by Lynn Maslen Kertell
pictures by Sue Hendra and John R. Maslen

Scholastic Inc.
New York • Toronto • London • Auckland • Sydney • Mexico City • New Delhi • Hong Kong • Buenos Aires

Ant

apple

Alligators eat apples.

Applesauce!

Bear

birds

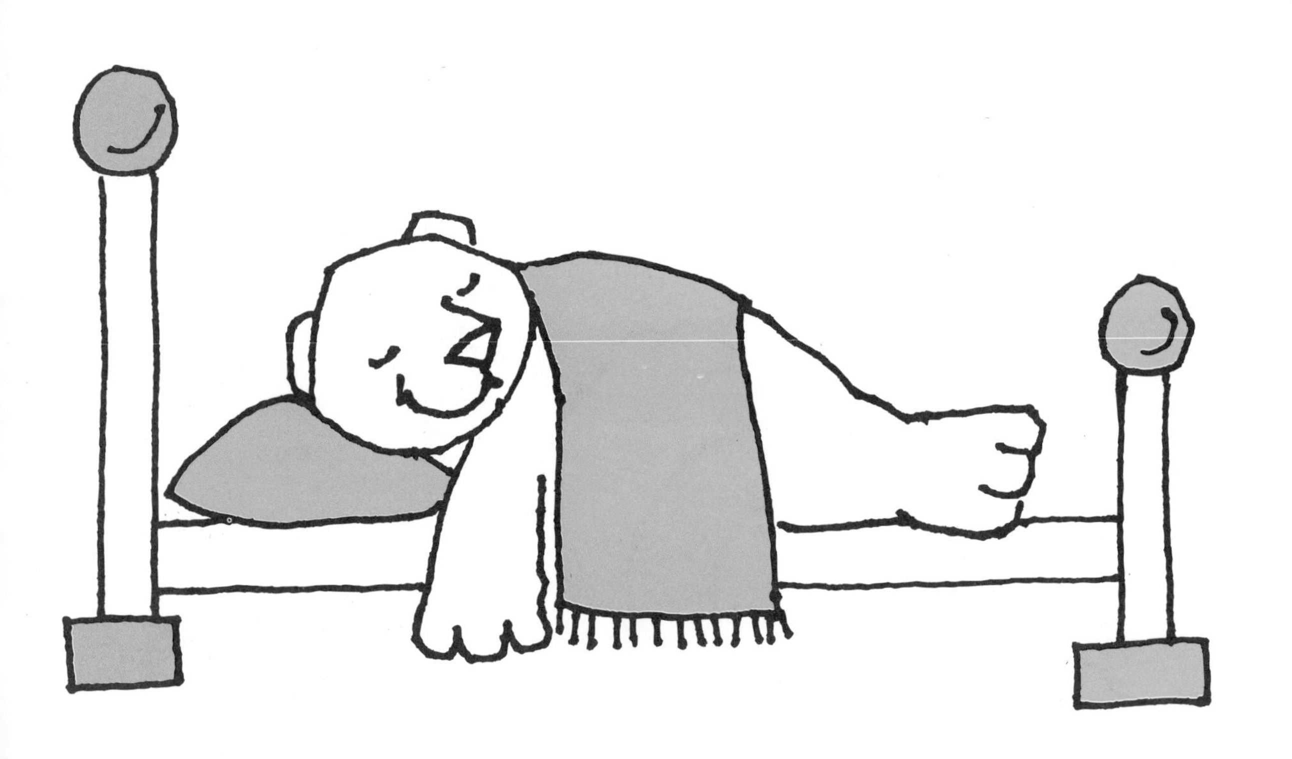

A blissful bear snoozes in bed.

Is there room for bunny and beaver?

Alligator serves breakfast.

Applesauce for all!

Look for these **a** and **b** words in this book.

all	bear
alligator(s)	beaver
ant	bed
apple(s)	birds
applesauce	blissful
	book
	breakfast
	bunny

Look for these additional **a** and **b** words in the pictures: antennae, apple tree, apron, ball, beaks, blanket, and bowls.